5117

Little Pig SAVES the SHIP

David Hyde Costello

ini Charlesbridge

For Indira

Published by Charlesbridge
85 Main Street
Watertown, MA 02472
(617) 926-0329
www.charlesbridge.com

Library of Congress Cataloging-in-Publication Data
Names: Costello, David, author, illustrator.
Title: Little Pig saves the ship / David Hyde Costello.
Description: Watertown, MA : Charlesbridge, [2017] | Summary: Little Pig is
     too small to go to sailing camp with his brothers and sisters, so his
     grandfather makes him a model ship, and together they sail it on the
     stream—until it gets carried away by the current, and Little Pig has to
     rescue the ship before it is wrecked.
Identifiers: LCCN 2016024028 (print) | LCCN 2016025259 (ebook) | ISBN
     9781580897150 | ISBN 9781607349297 (ebook) | ISBN 9781607349303 (ebook pdf)
Subjects: LCSH: Swine—Juvenile fiction. | Ship models—Juvenile fiction. |
     Fathers and sons—Juvenile fiction. | Brothers and sisters—Juvenile
     fiction. | CYAC: Pigs—Fiction. | Sailing—Fiction. | Fathers and
     sons—Fiction. | Brothers and sisters—Fiction.
Classification: LCC PZ7.C82283 Lk 2017 (print) | LCC PZ7.C82283 (ebook) |
DDC
     [E]—dc23
LC record available at https://lccn.loc.gov/2016024028

Printed in China
(hc) 10 9 8 7 6 5 4 3 2 1

Illustrations done in ink and watercolor on Strathmore cold-press watercolor paper
Display type created by Ryan O'Rourke and text type set in Palatino Sans Informal
Color separations by Colourscan Print Co Pte Ltd, Singapore
Printed by 1010 Printing International Limited in Huizhou, Guangdong, China
Production supervision by Brian G. Walker
Designed by Susan Mallory Sherman and Sarah Richards Taylor

Little Pig wished he could go to sailing camp with his brothers and sisters,

but he was too little.

Tiny, the oldest, had been to sailing camp five summers in a row. He gave Little Pig his book of sailors' knots and a piece of rope.

On the first day without his brothers and sisters,

Little Pig had a lot of spare time.

Grandpa and Poppy came over that night
to show Little Pig the beautiful ship
Poppy had started making for him.

On Sunday Little Pig sewed the sails, and
Poppy carved a little Poppy and a little
Little Pig to sail the ship.

They sailed the ship on Monday,

and on Tuesday,

and even in the rain on Wednesday.

On Thursday they built a dock.

On Friday they sailed the ship all the way across the stream.

But on Saturday a gust of wind blew
the ship into the current.

Little Pig waded in to grab the ship,

but the water was too deep for him.

Don't worry, Little Pig. I'll get her. You stay on land. It's slippery here and...

Little Pig saw a fallen tree. If he laid it across the stream, it would stop the ship.

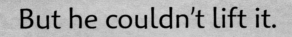

But he couldn't lift it.

Little Pig ran ahead of the current that carried the ship downstream.

GULP!

Maybe he could grab the ship as it
sailed under the bridge.

His arm was too short. He'd never
be able to reach the ship.

Then he remembered Tiny's rope
in his pocket!

I've almost got it!

Little Pig saved the ship!

When they got back to Little Pig's house, everyone was home from camp.

Little Pig still wished he could go sailing
with his brothers and sisters.